USBORNE
COUNTDOWN TO
Christmas

James Maclaine and Abigail Wheatley

Designed by
Eleanor Stevenson, Melissa Gandhi
and Tabitha Blore

Illustrated by
Flora Waycott, Helen Mackay,
Zoë Ingram and Clairice Gifford

GET READY FOR THE COUNTDOWN

Count down to Christmas from December 1 all the way to Christmas Eve. This book has exciting ideas for things for you to do EACH DAY.

Before you start, you'll need...

✓ paintbrush and liquid paints

✓ glue stick, tape and poster tack

✓ scissors and hole punch

✓ ruler

✓ old sponge

✓ string, ribbon and thread

✓ pencils and felt-tip pens

✓ red and green paper – and other colours too

✓ old newspapers, magazines and gift wrap

cardboard boxes, egg boxes and tubes

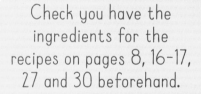

Check you have the ingredients for the recipes on pages 8, 16-17, 27 and 30 beforehand.

USBORNE QUICKLINKS For links to websites where you can find even more things to do in the days before Christmas, go to usborne.com/Quicklinks and type in the title of this book. Please follow the internet safety guidelines at Usborne Quicklinks. Children should be supervised online.

WRITE A LETTER TO SANTA

Copy this letter onto a piece of paper, filling in all the gaps with your own words.

Write your address in the top corner, so Santa knows where to deliver your presents.

Your home

List the presents you'd like. Choose carefully – Santa can't bring everything you want!

Dear Santa,

I hope you're feeling well at this very busy time of the year.

My name is ....

and I'm .... years old.

Please may I have any of these presents for Christmas?

....

....

....

Thank you very much.
All best wishes to you, the elves and the reindeer too,

Your name

Sign your name at the bottom.

Wait for DECEMBER 2 before you turn the page.

Doodle little pictures to decorate your letter.

3

23

DAYS TO GO...

CHRISTMAS DOVE

Make a flying dove by folding stiff rectangular paper.

Keep this strip.

1. Fold the paper like this. Cut off the bottom. Unfold the top...

2. Make a small fold from one corner. Fold again and again in the same direction.

3. Stop when you reach the middle. Draw on eyes, wings, legs and a beak.

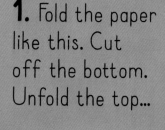

Keep the folds on the outside.

4. Bend the paper around, so the two pointed ends overlap.

5. Stick one point on top of the other with tape.

6. Cut the extra strip in half lengthways. Tape one piece over the join.

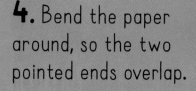

To fly your bird, hold it like this and throw firmly.

4

HOLLY WREATH

Follow these steps to make a wreath of holly leaves and berries from thin cardboard and paper.

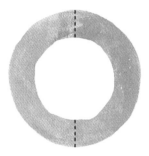

1. Draw around a plate on a piece of thin cardboard. Then, cut out the circle.

2. Fold the circle in half, then draw a big C shape against the fold.

3. Cut all the way along the line you drew. Then, unfold.

4. Get some green and red paper and draw shapes for holly leaves and berries. Cut them out and glue them on.

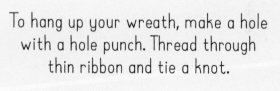

To hang up your wreath, make a hole with a hole punch. Thread through thin ribbon and tie a knot.

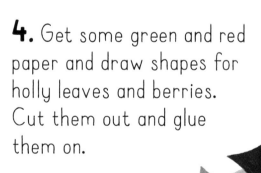

CHRISTMAS CARDS

Fold, cut and stick Christmas cards – and envelopes to go with them.

1. Fold a rectangle of thick, white paper in half for each card.

2. Cut a rectangle of colourful paper that's slightly smaller than your card. Fold it in half.

3. Draw one of these shapes on the colourful paper, next to the fold. Then, cut it out.

4. Unfold the rest of the paper and stick it on the front of the white card.

Snowman

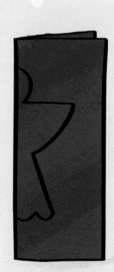

Fairy

Star

Happy Christmas!

Add details in pen, then write a message inside.

HOW TO MAKE ENVELOPES

You could turn gift wrap or pages from magazines into envelopes.

1. Cut out a big rectangle of paper and place the card on top, like this. Fold down the paper.

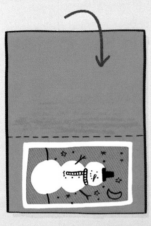

Leave a gap about 3cm (1 inch) wide on each side.

The rectangle needs to be about two and a half times taller than the card.

2. Turn over, then fold down the strip at the top.

3. Undo both folds. Then, fold in the left and right sides. Undo these folds too.

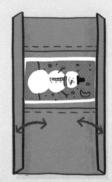

Make sure the folds are NOT too tight with the card.

4. Cut off these parts at each corner, along the creases.

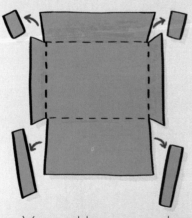

You could cut curved edges at both corners of the top flap.

5. Fold in the side flaps and stick the bottom flap on top.

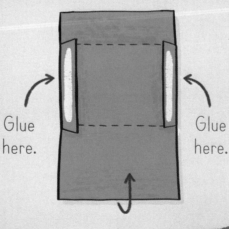

Glue here.

Glue here.

6. Slip the card inside. Then, stick down the top flap.

To make a label, cut out a shape and stick it on.

20

DAYS TO GO...

STAR SANDWICHES

Sandwiches look fun cut into stars, but you can use any shape of cookie cutter you can find.

YOU'LL NEED...

- a festive cookie cutter

- 2 slices of bread

- softened butter or plant-based spread

- sandwich fillings such as sliced cucumber or tomato, jam, chocolate spread, peanut butter or cheese

Eat up the leftover bread.

1. Cut as many shapes as you can from the bread.

2. Spread butter on one side of each shape.

3. Put some filling on half the shapes. Put the other shapes on top.

Eat them straight away, or wrap tightly and refrigerate.

You could use a small cutter to make a hole in some sandwich tops.

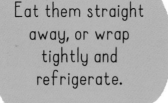

TREE SPINNER

This paper spiral makes the shape of a Christmas tree as it spins.

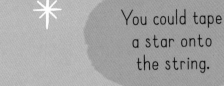

You could tape a star onto the string.

1. Draw around a bowl on some old gift wrap. Cut out the circle.

2. Draw a spiral on top. Cut along this line.

3. Make a hole in the middle with a hole punch. Thread a long piece of string through the hole. Tie a knot at one end.

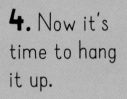

4. Now it's time to hang it up.

Blow gently so it spins.

PRINT GIFT WRAP

Make printing stamps from cardboard, then print patterns on big pieces of newspaper or brown paper.

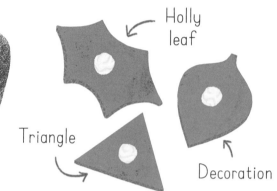

Holly leaf

Triangle

Decoration

1. Cut out different shapes from cardboard. Stick balls of poster tack on top for handles.

2. Squirt some paint onto an old plate. Spread it out with a paintbrush.

3. Press your stamp into the paint gently, then make prints.

4. Add more paint to the stamp whenever the prints start to fade. Then, wait for them all to dry.

There are lots of ideas for prints on the next page.

You could print at random...

Print three overlapping triangles to make tree shapes like these...

...or make rows of prints.

Scrunch paper into a ball and use it to print big spots.

These prints were made with a short branch from a real Christmas tree.

To print snow, press bubble wrap in white paint.

LITTLE PENGUINS

You'll need half a potato and the top of a carrot to print penguins.
Dry them with paper towel before you start...

1. Press the potato stamp in black paint and print a body.

2. Wait for it to dry before pressing the carrot in white paint to print a tummy.

3. Use a thin brush to paint on eyes, a beak, wings and feet.

17

DAYS TO GO...

PAPER CHAINS

Cut up different types of paper into strips. Then, make chains of loops and hearts.

1. Cut lots of long, thin strips of paper.

2. Tape the ends of a strip together, to make a loop.

3. Thread another strip through and tape its ends together to start a chain.

4. Keep on adding loops.

5. To add a heart-shaped link, fold a strip in half.

6. Unfold it and bend in the ends so they're close to each other.

7. Tape both ends together.

8. Thread another strip through the heart, to continue the chain.

You could alternate hearts and loops.

STAR MOBILE

For this mobile you'll need a star-shaped cookie cutter - or use any festive cookie cutter. You'll also need a stick, thread and some shiny paper.

1. Put your cookie cutter on shiny paper or gift wrap. Draw around it using a pencil.

2. Move the cutter and draw around it again. Do this lots of times. Cut out the shapes.

Tie a knot at the end.

3. Make a hole in the point of each shape with a hole punch.

4. Poke a long piece of thread through the hole.

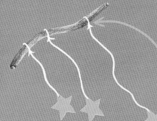

Tie on all the stars, like this.

5. Tie the other end of the thread to your stick.

6. Cut a long piece of thread. Tie it to each end of the stick.

PAPER DECORATIONS

You can cut shapes from thin cardboard and decorate them with scraps of bright paper or gift wrap.

1. On some thin cardboard, draw shapes like these, but bigger. Cut them out.

2. Tear up brightly coloured paper or gift wrap into lots of pieces.

3. Glue them all over the shapes – front and back if you like. Trim the edges.

4. You could glue on ribbon to make stripes, like this.

5. Make a hole at the top using a hole punch. Tie on thread for hanging.

14

STICK DECORATIONS

To make these decorations, use ice lolly sticks or cut out strips of cardboard.

1. For Santa, paint the top and bottom of a stick red. Let it dry.

2. Use a pen to draw on eyes, a nose and a belt.

3. Cut a beard and hat trim from white paper. Glue them on.

4. Tape a loop of thread to the back.

For an elf, use green paint and red paper shapes.

For Rudolph, stick on a paper tummy, muzzle, ears and antlers. Draw on a face.

For a snowman, paint the entire stick white. Stick on a paper hat, nose and scarf.

15

13

DAYS TO GO...

BREADSTICK REINDEER

You can make these nibbles using breadsticks, knot-shaped pretzels, chocolate and sweets.

YOU'LL NEED...

- 4 tablespoons of chocolate chips
- around 6 pretzels
- 3 breadsticks
- 18 little round sweets
- black or brown writing icing
- ...and some baking parchment

1. Melt the chocolate in a heatproof bowl over a pan of hot water. Leave until the chocolate melts. Take the bowl off the pan wearing oven gloves.

2. Cut each pretzel in half. Don't worry if it breaks.

Use clean scissors.

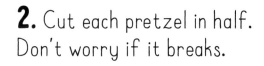

You want two pieces roughly like this.

Eat any leftover bits.

3. Break each breadstick in half. Put parchment on a board.

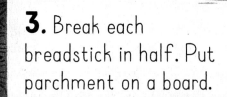

4. Dip the rounded end of a breadstick in the melted chocolate. Put it on the board.

5. Push two pretzel pieces into the chocolate, like this.

Add two sweets for eyes here...

...and a sweet for a nose here.

6. Make the rest in the same way. Chill for ten minutes, so the chocolate sets.

7. Dot on writing icing for the eyes.

If you want to make more of us, double all the amounts.

LITTLE TREES

Make little Christmas trees using cardboard egg boxes and green paint. You'll need one large egg box, or two small ones, for each tree.

You need four of these cone shapes to make a tree.

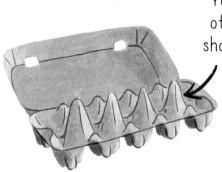

1. Open an egg box. Cut around the bottom of the sticking-up parts.

2. Trim the bases so they sit flat.

3. Paint them green. Let them dry.

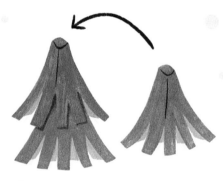

4. Cut slits halfway up the sides. Then, bend them out a little.

5. Stack them on top of each other, like this.

If you make more, you could paint them different greens.

11

DAYS TO GO...

SNOWFLAKE DECORATION

You'll need a long cardboard tube, plus glue and thread, to make this festive decoration.

Glue here.

1. Press the tube flat then cut off twelve loop-shaped strips. Each one needs to be about as wide as your finger.

2. Open out six of the loops a little. Glue two together, like this.

3. Glue on four more, so it looks like a snowflake. Let the glue dry.

4. Fold all the remaining loops in half, like this.

Glue here.

5. Glue both sides of each folded shape onto the snowflake. Let it dry.

Tie thread through one of the loops to hang it up.

19

FESTIVE FINGERPRINTING

Make a fingerprinting kit with an old sponge and some liquid paints. Then, print Christmassy pictures or cards.

1. Cut the sponge into pieces for different colours. Brush thin layers of paint on top.

2. Press a finger into the paint, then onto paper. Clean your finger with paper towel before changing colours.

3. After the paint has dried, you can draw on top with a black pen.

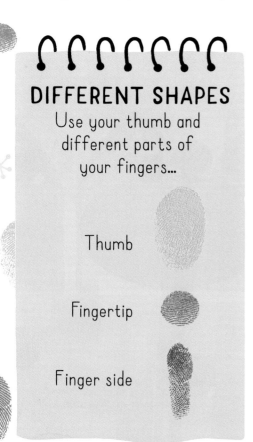

DIFFERENT SHAPES
Use your thumb and different parts of your fingers...

Thumb

Fingertip

Finger side

YOU COULD PRINT...

DECORATIONS
Draw shapes like these and fill them with fingerprints.

STOCKINGS
Make two overlapping prints with your thumb. Then, draw on patterns.

CHRISTMAS LIGHTS
Draw a looping line between lots of fingerprints.

Draw on faces, arms, buttons, hats and scarves.

SNOWMEN
Make white fingerprints on blue paper.

REINDEER
Print each reindeer's body first, then use your fingertip to print its head.

You could decorate a card with fingerprints.

Turn to page 7 if you want to make an envelope.

SANTA'S BEARD

Follow the steps below for curling strips of paper. Then, make a picture of Santa with a 3D curly beard.

Curl strips with a ruler...

Place the ruler's narrow edge on a strip, near one end. Press down firmly.

Then, carefully pull the strip all the way through.

...or with a pencil.

Place your pencil across the strip.

Then, roll the pencil to wrap the paper around it tightly.

Let go and remove the pencil.

Glue here.

1. Draw Santa's face on some paper, like this. Stick on a red triangle for his hat.

2. Curl lots of white strips. Dab glue on the back of the curls to stick them in rows under Santa's nose.

GIFT TAGS

You can make gift tags to label presents. It's best to write messages on the tags before you attach them with tape.

1. Draw circles, triangles or other shapes onto thick paper, then cut them out.

2. Make a hole in each shape using a hole punch. Push thread through the hole and tie a knot.

3. Now it's time to decorate them!

Make round tags by drawing around a cup.

To add a polar bear, tear a shape from white paper for its head. Glue it on, then draw its face and ears.

Dot snowy white paint on a triangular tag.

You could make a pair of tags shaped like mittens.

For a tree tag, stick on three overlapping green triangles. Paint on decorations.

SNOWY HOUSE

This 'gingerbread house' is made from brown cardboard and white paint. It even stands up on its own.

1. Cut a big rectangle from brown cardboard.

2. Cut off the top corners, like this.

3. Draw on windows, a door and other details in pencil. Then, go over the lines in white paint.

You could copy the picture on the next page.

It needs to be around half as tall as the house.

4. Cut a triangle from cardboard. Fold it in half.

5. Glue one half to the back of your house, like this, to stand it up.

You could make more than one house for a village.

6
DAYS TO GO...

MINI LANTERNS

These lanterns are really easy to make using bright paper.

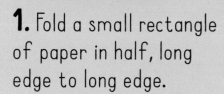

1. Fold a small rectangle of paper in half, long edge to long edge.

2. Leave a gap at the top as wide as your thumb and draw a line across.

3. Make lots of cuts up to this line. Leave gaps as wide as your finger between them and at both ends.

4. Unfold. Spread glue down one of the short edges, then join both together.

5. Cut a long, thin strip of paper. Glue both ends inside the top for a handle.

You could draw patterns on the top and bottom before step 4.

26

REINDEER FOOD

Make this before Christmas Eve, so you can leave it out for Rudolph and his friends. Use or leave out whichever ingredients you like.

YOU COULD USE...

- cereal such as rice crispies, cornflakes or multigrain hoops

- shelled, unsalted nuts

- pumpkin or sunflower seeds

- chocolate chips

- dried fruit such as raisins, cranberries, figs or pitted dates

1. If you're using big figs or dates, cut them into small pieces using clean scissors.

2. Put a handful of each of your chosen ingredients in a bowl.

3. Mix everything together well. Store in an airtight container.

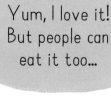

Yum, I love it! But people can eat it too...

4

DAYS TO GO...

DECORATE GIFTS

You could wrap presents in plain paper and then add finishing touches like these.

Give gifts faces. You could stick on shapes and draw on details for a bear or snowman.

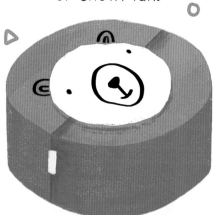

This gift looks as if it's covered in tree lights. First wrap string around a few times before tying a knot.

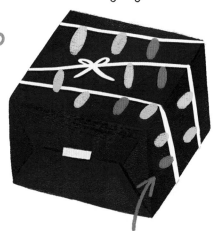

Then, stick light shapes next to the string.

To make rosettes, snip again and again into the edges of paper circles – or leftover cupcake cases.

Make a tree shape by gluing on strips that get bigger from top to bottom.

You could stick smaller rosettes on top.

Add a square for the tree trunk.

ELF HAT

You can pretend to be one of Santa's elves with this green and white paper hat.

Cut the string so both ends meet.

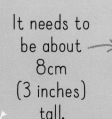

It needs to be about 8cm (3 inches) tall.

You could cut out triangle shapes along the top for a zigzag edge.

1. Use string to measure around your head, above your ears.

2. Cut a strip of thick paper, about 3cm (1 inch) longer than the string.

3. Fold the string in half, then cut out a square of thick paper the same length.

4. Copy this hat shape and cut it out.

5. Draw around a small jar on some paper twice. Cut out both circles.

6. Glue down the hat in the middle of the strip. Glue its tip onto one circle and glue the other circle on top.

7. Stick the ends of the strip together to make a loop. Now your hat is ready to wear...

CHRISTMASSY ORANGES

Use oranges and spike-shaped spices called cloves to make these decorations. They're for smelling, not eating – they fill the air with the scent of Christmas.

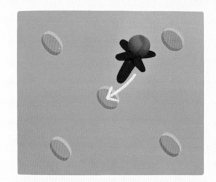

1. Use a pencil to pierce holes in the skin of each orange. Leave gaps between the holes.

2. Push the pointed end of a clove into every hole you made.

3. Put them in a warm, dry place where you can smell them as you pass by.

You could use your cloves to make different patterns, like these.